D1716667

COLD TURKEY

Also by Mac Hammond

The Horse Opera and Other Poems

COLD TURKEY

MAC HAMMOND

THE SWALLOW PRESS INC.

CHICAGO

Published by
The Swallow Press Incorporated
1139 South Wabash Avenue
Chicago, Illinois 60605

LIBRARY OF CONGRESS CATALOG CARD NUMBER   76-81964

Grateful acknowledgment is made to these periodicals
in which the poems noted first appeared:
The London Observer, "The Robot"
Choice, "The Florist"

The recording of "The Holidays" included in this
volume was recorded by Mr. Hammond and produced
by Michael J. DiNoto and Joseph W. Romanowski
at the music laboratories of the State University of
New York at Buffalo. The publishers wish to acknowl-
edge the partial financial subsidy from the Research
Council of the State University of New York, which
made possible the inclusion of the record.

for Ross and Anna, so they will know
what it was like

THE HOLIDAYS

SCIENCE FICTION

RIGHT TURN ONLY

SAME TIME SAME PLACE

THE DAYS OF THE WEEK

I

THE HOLIDAYS

VALENTINE'S DAY

It comes through the mail slot,
An envelope, addressed to you,
The postage stamp Lincoln or, now,
Is it Johnson, cancelled out
With a motto *Have A Heart, Fight*
Multiple Sclerosis or *Heart Disease*.
The flap is glued tight and you pry it
Open, with a fingernail, broken.
Your heart's a - flutter as you pull out
The Valentine; it's pink and gaudy and
Just to your taste — lace and
Cupids around a stabbed heart,
Bleeding. And there's no signature,
Just BE MY VALENTINE, TOOTS—
And you come in a blaze of dreams:
A fan, a distant admirer, one
Who loves your body more than
Life, your wife, your daughter,
The mailman, the milkman, the
Milkmaid, the butcher, the baker,
The lady upstairs, the Lady. . . .

EASTER

Eggs, the whole family — Sister and Mother,
Junior and Dad — dipped and painted
With vegetable dyes — oranges and greens,
Purple and red, a few decalled
With funny faces and new-born chicks,
All laid out on the kitchen table, in baskets,
Ready for the Easter Bunny to hide.
The children go to bed and Mother
And Dad hide them — all in the living-
Room, under chairs, on window ledges,
Nestled in potted plants, and a couple,
For the little one, out in plain sight.
And they go off to bed, both strangely
Excited. They dream of golf. Morning
Comes and the children are risen, up
To hunt them, collecting the hard-boiled eggs
One-by-O there's one, I found one, into nests
Of green paper grass. He or she who finds
The most wins — what? because they all go
Back to the kitchen and, day after day, are
Eaten, in salad sandwiches.

FOURTH OF JULY

At the Commons, Baseball Park or
Riverside, huge crowds gather at dusk,
Sitting on blankets, on camp chairs, some
On the ground, babies and grandmas,
The well and ill — everybody hot
And sweaty, balloons on strings, flag
Up the flagpole — ready to watch
The local county 4th-of-July annual
Fireworks display. The first rocket up,
Amid applause, is aerial bombs, one!
Two! three! Kids, the little ones, cry,
As an avalanche of stars sprays the sky
For twenty minutes. On the ground
The ground flunkies punk and pop
Roman candles and fizz out
St. Catherine wheels, building up
To the grand finale — flash
Bombs bursting in air,
More rockets' red glare, waterfalls
On both sides of Old Glory, burning,
Burning — red, white, and blue —
For a moment only, as nobody
Believes it will
In the great nick of time.

HALLOWEEN

The butcher knife goes in, first, at the top
And carves out the round stemmed lid,
The hole of which allows the hand to go
In to pull the gooey mess inside, out —
The walls scooped clean with a spoon.
A grim design decided on, that afternoon,
The eyes are the first to go,
Isosceles or trapezoid, the square nose,
The down-turned mouth with three
Hideous teeth and, sometimes,
Round ears. At dusk it's
Lighted, the room behind it dark.
Outside, looking in, it looks like a
Pumpkin, it looks like ripeness
Is all. Kids come, beckoned by
Fingers of shadows on leaf-strewn lawns
To trick or treat. Standing at the open
Door, the sculptor, a warlock, drops
Penny candies into their bags, knowing
The message of winter: only the children,
Pretending to be ghosts, are real.

THANKSGIVING

for George and Marilyn Hochfield

The man who stands above the bird, his knife
Sharp as a Turkish scimitar, first removes
A thigh and leg, half the support
On which the turkey used to stand. This
Leg and thigh he sets aside on an extra
Plate. All his weight now on
One leg, he lunges for the wing, the wing
On the same side of the bird from which
He has just removed the leg and thigh.
He frees the wing enough to expose
The breast, the wing not severed but
Collapsed down to the platter. One hand
Holding the fork, piercing the turkey
Anywhere, he now begins to slice the breast,
Afflicted by small pains in his chest,
A kind of heartburn for which there is no
Cure. He serves the hostess breast, her
Own breast rising and falling. And so on,
Till all the guests are served, the turkey
Now a wreck, the carver, exhausted, a
Mere carcass of his former self. Everyone
Says thanks to the turkey carver and begins
To eat, thankful for the cold turkey
And the Republic for which it stands.

CHRISTMAS

for Svatava Pirkova-Jakobson

The whole family decks the Christmas tree.
Father brings it in, fussing and cussing
At the standard, and, finally, hoists it up
To the ceiling, and says Ooh and Aah. Everyone
Says Ooh and Aah and Mother throws a sheet
Around the base, down on all fours
To adjust the snow around the waterpot.
The kids open ornament boxes, the girls attach
Hangers and the boys hang balls on the
Boughs, red and blue and green, big ones
And little ones. The girls, giggling,
Circle the tree and lay on garlands of popcorn-
Cranberry wreaths. Mother tests the lights
And, with Father's help, spirals them up to the
Top. Everyone stands back and throws
Tinsel. At last, the angel hair, the lights
Are plugged in and the whole thing lights up like a
Christmas tree, the tiny star at the tippy-tip-top
Gleaming like a. . .

NEW YEAR'S

for Norman O. Brown

The children stay up, a few friends
Come over for the annual pink champagne
And dead piglet, not served, of course,
Till the New Year, when, on TV,
The Times Square crowds go manic.
At midnight, everybody sees Father Time
Descending the staircase. He looks like
The host, back from the john, besotted,
Glass in hand, and dressed in the shroud
Of a size forty-eight Shetland jacket,
Who passes out on the sofa he's so
Smashed by the cup of kindness. Everybody
Sees the Baby in his face, so peaceful
In sleep he's not even awakened
By the croaking of Auld Lang Syne
Or the hand-ratchet noisemakers meant to dispel
The dead of winter and welcome the spring.

II

SCIENCE FICTION

THE MAD SCIENTIST

for Roman Jakobson

This morning, ever since breakfast,
With a scheme in my head, my radioactive
Mind clicks like a Geiger-counter.
I am manic again. The Maniac loose
In his laboratory. My fingers play
With the dials of my electromagnetic
Thingamajig, while in Florence-flasks
Liquids effervesce. I could blow up
The world. My assistant says "Doctor"
And I remember who I am and why I am
Here this morning, my scheme to talk,
Communicate with a Creature From Outer Space.
My earth-bound colleagues bore me.
How much I could learn from a creature
Not of this planet, how to soar in the galaxies
And live forever. I seek Superior Knowledge.
So, I must find how to say *I love you*
In Martian, before they come, again,
To take me, jacketed and screaming, away.

THE ROBOT

Of course I drink, I smoke too much
But how would you like it to be bound
By a memory bank, compulsions
Built in, arms and legs of lead,
A head of iron, for eyes, aluminum slits,
For heart, a high-speed computer.
I move through the day like a vacuum
Cleaner, and everything I say or do
I learned by ribbon or by rote.
At eight and eight I take my pills
And, day and night, am tranquil.
But I was built to serve the universe,
Attuned to the workings of the stars.
So how, these days, can I be content
Merely to circle and circle about
In no direction. My psychiatrist says
I cannot untangle the wires of my past
Or put together a future. I am sick
Of his counsel. Oh, only to live in the present
And write one poem better than Baudelaire!

THE CREATURE FROM OUTER SPACE

I move upon the earth, invisible,
What you call a ghost, nor could you bear
To see me naked as I am. I am half
Mouth. From inter-stellar space I come
With X-ray eyes to see through all of you
And what I see appalls. You, who scrawled
That filthy picture on the toilet stall,
You, unfaithful to the wife and kids
In your imagination; you, who jacks
His seed into a handkerchief, and you
And you and you! I swear the earth
Crawls with sexual dissatisfactions.

III

RIGHT TURN ONLY

My mother, flapping behind the steering-wheel
Of her 1931 blue convertible Ford
With rumble-seat and yellow wicker-wire spokes,
Came to a

On her way to play at bridge
And declaim, over diamonds and hearts,
And in between prohibited gin Swiss Itches
(Straight down the gullet
And, for chaser, lemon
And, then, salt) her recent uncontested
Divorce.

My always angry father, roaring, drunk-driving
His new 1946 black Packard coupe, passed at 90

a

Just before the anti-freeze-full radiator
Fell back, ripping against the fan.
But not even that could slow him down,
Or sober him up.

My poor, ever-loving sister had three

And, every day, drove them very fast
In her grey, air-conditioned, this year's
Chrysler four-door sedan, to and from

a
SLOW

END
CONSTRUCTION

IV

SAME TIME SAME PLACE

THE EDITORIAL OFFICE

It's all right to let him publish now.
We've kept him out of it ten years,
Given as he was to romantic lyric
And those elegies, lovely, but so dumb
In the face of death.   Yes, let him publish.
He's been through a lot, death of his wife,
Three times in a sanitarium, a change
Of sex, weather-beaten.   He looks like
Rimbaud would have at sixty, *deréglement*,
Gaga. But his new poems, now,
That's different, as different as
Trick is from trick.   Look where he comes.
Draw the arras.   He composes with his prick.

THE SUPERMARKET

for Davenport Brown

The hungry pass an electric eye
And a glass door opens automatically.
Each pushes a grocery cart, up and down
The aisles. The autumn harvest is in:
Stacks of bags of potatoes, six counts
Of pears, frosty pumpkins, warty
Squash, red and purple Indian corn. And
The autumn slaughter: pork chops,
Legs of lamb, hamburger, calves' brains,
All done up in cellophane, marked
With weight and price to the penny and the ounce.
Canned goods by the ton: Campbell's, Hunt's,
Delmonte, beans, peas, beets, olives
From Spain, invite the shades of starved
Young men, women, and children, who
Roam the market, hands in their
Broken pockets, hands on the bloat
Of their guts, it's beriberi, it's
Rickets, malnutrition, they reach out,
Their skinny arms, for vitamins, for
Starch, for anything, food. They never
Get to the check-out counter, never
Win the bread or bring home the bacon,

They are lost forever, among the plenty,
Limping up and down the aisles, even
When the store is closed, closed as it is
To them, their slack mouths, the wealth
Still, and it will always be, undistributed.

THE BANK

The doors open at nine. The rich descend
To safety deposit vaults to clip and cash in
Coupons and hoard jewels. I go to a teller
Who tells me about a teller, Retig, who
Fled with a bundle, now serving double
Time in Attica, New York. I submit my paycheck,
Just enough to pay off payments, not a cent
For savings. O, I want to rob the bank,
All the money they make on money. I want
To visit, on visiting day, Carl Retig,
Find out how to do it, stuff small bills
In a bag, fly to Rio, to Peru, not be able
To spend so much in a day as I make
With money. And, if I'm nabbed by the FBI,
Caught napping, think of all the poems
I could read and re-read and write
In a federal prison, the rest of my life:
My *Ballad of Ossining Jail*, *Surreal Penitentiary
Poems*, *Poems from the Clink*, *Pen Poems
For Pen Pals*, and, at last, my *Apocalypse!*

A SOUTH SEA ISLAND

Especially when after the white snow
Piles up and a snow of city soot
Grays it and it turns to slush
And the gray slush mirrors the gray sky
And the avenue trees are black and naked,
I want to go where it is always Spring,
A South Sea Island, or any island paradise,
Like Gauguin, go native, maybe even paint
A little, an easel set up on the salt-sea beach,
Polynesian beauties, stripped to the waist,
Surround me, hibiscus and breadfruit,
Manaò tupapaú, Spirit of the Dead
Watching. Of course, I will never go, son
Of a cold climate, will never abandon
Wife, dogs, house, children, life
Here at The University, love. But
The idea plays on in my mind like a movie,
And impels, like the swell of the sea
Grand romantic gestures, that freeze
In my poems, raw ice dangling at the eaves.

THE DUMP

It all depends on what you think of it,
A big city dump: enough to feed an Asian,
Or an African, state: mostly cardboard, paper
(Trees) and tincans (veins of natural zinc).
The city fathers burn it, but not before gulls
Alight and tug 'n tatter the shards
Of the culture. Looked at one way it's
Metaphor: one thing like another, a
Bedspring (love), a mattress (tumbling).
Nothing grows here, nothing takes root
And, yet, all the junk cries out for
A poet, because all the parts make a whole,
A dump. Looked at, this metonymic way,
A metonymic poet could say: this garbage
Stands for us, what we left behind,
The agony of unwrapping, the brown paper,
The string, the gummed label, what
It meant to discover, inside the box,
A gift, the great gift we, as children, had wanted.

THE SYMPHONY

I usually sleep like a Philistine
Dragged there by his wife, drugged
With the business of poems in my head,
Waiting for intermission, to get down
To the bar for a beer or whiskey.
During Brahms, my soul-master,
I doze, dreaming of Dvořák, his *New World
Symphony*, or, during Schubert, my god,
I drift to a plateau of gauchos
Riding the pampas to a water-hole.
Once, I awakened: Bach's *Fifth
Piano Concerto*, the second movement cantaline,
That afternoon you played it, *in memoriam*,
For Kennedy. I wept and went home:
Wept, because no poem could say it;
Went home, because that was the place
To go, the place — how shall I say it —
Where I could put it, again and again, on the gramophone.

THE DENTIST

You sit there, bibbed, a gift horse,
While the dentist peeks and pokes with
Sharp instruments, looking for cavities.
Aha, the left back molar, already half
Silver, has a hole the size of a pea;
But, to your tongue, feel, it's a canyon,
An absessed abyss that looks back
And says *decay*. Dear Doctor Dentist,
Plug with porcelain, silver, and gold;
Drill with your high-speed jack-hammer drill;
And (remember the lurid X-rays you took?)
Preserve my teeth, my chompers,
Stained with nicotine and all the dirty
Words I have, again, to say about death.

THE MOVIES

At the ticket kiosk you buy tickets for two
And, at the door, the first usher tears them
In two, dropping half in his counting stand,
The other half in your palm.   Your date
Goes in first, downstairs to the john, while
You buy popcorn and jujyfruits at the popcorn counter.
Here you are, in a palace — gold leaf
Spread on the buttocks of putti
So far up in the mezzanine vault they look like
Angels, who will never come down
To sit on the carved-back chairs
Or walk on the nouveau carpet.
You are prince of the evening, and, once
In your seats, you re-live a fairy tale:
Boy meets Girl; Frankenstein, the Wolf Man;
Ginger Rogers, Fred Astaire; John Wayne,
A bullet; and, then, after the Looney Tunes
And the newsreel, you glance once more
At the queer, next you, restless
In his seat and "READY FOR SEX" as he scrawled,
In violet ink, at the urinal; and, then, you
Move up the aisle, out to the cold,

Long walk back with your girl, who
Deigns one single kiss at the door.
Alone, walking home, looking up at the stars,
The stars spell out a message: *the snow
Is a virgin, the youth pined away with desire.*

THE THEATER

for Albert Cook

The house lights dim. The curtain opens:
Orestes has returned to avenge his father.
He and Electra do it, butcher Aegisthus
And, so a messenger says, murder their mother.
The lights go up and, here we are in a box
Circle, the theater quite like the palace
Of Atreus, Greek anyway, two Graces
Supporting the proscenium arch, two
Satyrs glaring down at the orchestra;
And, as we leave, clutching our souvenir
Programs, toothless Erinyes pursue, because we,
Children of quarrelsome fathers and mothers,
Are always pleased, whatever we say, to have
This dirty work done for us in a dream or a play.

THE FLORIST

I wish I could say it with flowers,
A poem about flowers: carnations
Or violets, nouns: snapdragons, verbs;
Whole sentences of heather. Or, I wish
My muse, that old bitch, were a flower,
A green chrysanthemum or a blue-black rose.
I remember, first time in the madhouse,
I finger-fucked a whole bouquet
Of flame-red dahlias. The attendants were amazed.
Even sane, I love flowers and can
Gaze at poinsettias for hours. For me,
The hyacinth still says *alas*,
And a pale narcissus reminds me of death.

THE LIQUOR STORE

When I am old, shivering, and confined,
At least, to a wheelchair, by the fire,
I will want whiskey, even as now,
Run out on a New Year's Eve, alone, I dream
Of the shut-down place where they sell it:
Rows of bottles brim full of the South —
Kentucky Tavern, *Virginia Gentleman*, straight
And sour mash, aged eight full years in oak.
I wonder what I would do, when old,
If broke, I could not buy whiskey?
Would I be sober and go, laughing
To the grave? Whiskey, spare me,
Think of all the truth I have told
Drunk on Barleycorn, think of all
The poems I wrote half-stoned,
Half out of my mind, and the dances
I danced around the thyrsus. Dionysus,
When I am old and crying for whiskey,
Bless all places where whiskey is sold.
O, pickle me stiff against the stiffening cold.

THE FILLING STATION

Because, Saturdays, they broadcast the Met,
I drive the old bus, often, in, to Texaco,
For a wash, lube job, and change of Havoline.
Hydraulically up on an indoor jack, they
Squirt her joints with grease and drain
Her crankcase; then, down, down, she comes
For a sponge-bath of soap and wax-in water.
Now the old car purrs like new, her spark-
Plugs pointed, her wheels aligned, her
Handles tight, her tight brakes loose,
All ready for High-Test and anti-freeze.

At the double row of Sky-Chief pumps,
The handsome man who wears the star
Really gases her.

THE DRUG STORE

You can read, there, the culture, our obsession
With hair and physical beauty, our sweet-tooth,
Our wealth of choice and indecisions. A drug store is
A polyphony of beautiful names for our needs
(Give me an ounce of civet, good apothecary,
To sweeten my tongue): cocaine, cola, fingernail
Polish remover, Pertussin, Milk of Magnesia, Tums,
Noxema, Kodak, Vicks, Vitalis, Mum. . . .

THE MUSEUM
The Black Judges of Hell

All six or eight are so black and terrific,
The curators, or maybe the guards, of Toronto's
Royal Ontario Museum have put them apart,
One each to a room, where they preside,
Brooding over tomb-tiles, funerary figures,
And all the other, mostly elegant, junk
From four millenia of Chinese culture.
The judges, each about three feet high,
Are 15th century Ming iron, *noir*, as I said,
Each but two are seated, and each
Not so much a symbol of law and order as,
Simply, civilized, with robes falling
To the floor, in *l'art nouveau* folds,
Hands hidden, small pill-box hat
Flat on the head. Where, when, for what dead
Cult of the dead were they placed all together
In rows or semi-circle? Perhaps, all together,
They prove evil.

        Someday, they will meet
Again, all together, not in any museum,
But, there, where the darkest evil is,

Say, after the next world slaughter,
When Chinese troops put poets and poets'
Sons to work in a mine and that mine
Is a one-way, no exit entrance to a hell you cannot imagine.

A FUNERAL

The family sits aside, in a booth-box
Reserved for them, the widow sobbing,
The son holding back tears, the daughter
Peaceful in her sure belief in God —
All hidden, by a veil, from the friends
And colleagues of the dead man. The pall-
Bearers bear the casket in, to the chapel
Of a Hickman Avenue branch of the Dunn
Funeral Parlor, while the Hammond
Shrills out a voluntary. The pastor
Says a few words about life everlasting;
The congregation sings *Nearer, My God*
And, then, files past the coffin for a last
Look. Alone, the family goes, a group, to say
Goodbye, and the prodigal stoops over
To kiss the corpse, finding his father's lips
As hard and cold as ever, as hard and
Cold as the marble sets in the sockets
Of the eyes, sent, after death, to the
Capitol City Eye Bank where they live
On, staring and mindless. Outside,
The fat black limousines cue up for
The long ride, out to the cemetery,

Headlights dimmed by the daylight.
At the family plot, ashes and roses,
Regrets and all the dreams of yesterday
Are lowered, on pulleys, into a 3 by 6 foot grave.

V

THE DAYS OF THE WEEK

MONDAY

The baskets of towels left by the curl-chested lover
Are washed in the mountain stream and dried in the light
Of the mid-day moon. The washerwoman, fed on buttered bread,
Remembers the snuggling on the sheets and carries in her womb
The blunt-headed seeds and aches. Her back breaks from
Washing and all her body is limp from
Him who thrusts upon her the weight of love.
Such a woman, her fair face turned to the moon's tide,
Must have been my great grandmother, on the German,
The paternal side, a name lost,
Now, to some unknown Ohio grave,
Her husband a cobbler, the same whose
Tools I display on the mantel, antiques
For which I have no use, next to his picture,
A daguerreotype, a mere boy in puffed shirt-sleeves,
My great grandfather, whose name I do know,
Jakob, a murderer. I am so nervous. It must be
The sins of the fathers. It is him I must blame.
But my heart reaches out to that woman
Who did his wash on Monday, the moon's day,
Her life and the triumph of her broken sorrow.

TUESDAY

My graceful string bean sister naked lay, when she was ten,
A Tuesday, under mother's ironing board. The iron
Slid off and seared her tight-lipped crotch. There was a rush
To have the burns anointed, an ambulance
Sirened through the streets and, in EMERGENCY,
The interns performed a laying on of hands.
She did not whimper even when a nurse re-wound
Her wounds nor cry out to family visitors
Her pain — "A little soldier," so my father said.
Well, to make the long story short, she married,
Had three sons, lived well and long, died
An easy death; but no man — husband, son, or brother —
Since that cauterizing fire fell from Mars or Tiw,
Ever satisfied her deep-down central pleasures.

WEDNESDAY

My father, a mercurial merchant, told me
About flowers and, once, about sex, the fool,
He made a vegetable soup the like of which
No cook ever made again. He did not love me
And I am full of woe because he did not love me.
At the ripe age of 42 I wish to mend
What was torn between us. Dad, where are you?
I am mad with that question, "wōd" as Chaucer
Used to say.
And my father is dead, in a grave,
And I am a father, my son looks up to me, I
Slap him for talking back. Father, son, let's
Begin again. Let's go out to a valley, farms
Around, green grass and crimson clover,
Bees, and little animals benign, owls
Blinking, lay ourselves out beside a stream,
Naked, look at one another, each man-root
A man-root, lounge, in love with one another.
Come back, father, little son, what I offer
Is just, is just human. Oh, Wednesday falls
Again. I am back, O, I am back where I began.
I can't stand it. Father, son, how many times,
Between coming and going, must I call and call?

THURSDAY

Thursday, 1924, Thor let fling his hammer:
The Hammonds, Mott and Esther, gave regular birth
To my baby sister. They had agreed to name her,
From some magazine of starlets, Jerry Lou. Grandma
Prepared a dinner — roast beef with gravy. The platter
Clattered to the new-scrubed floor; the baby fell
From the slimy hands of the doctor against a door.
Jerry Lou died two days after. Esther, mother,
Lay abed, time on her hands, each hour seemed an hour;
Eternity strolled around her room. The nurse,
An angel, held her hand, theologized, and read,
From Scripture, the *Apocalypse*. Both Jerry Lou and mother,
Time told before the twinkling had far, O so far to go.

FRIDAY

She is the wife of the king of gods, fish-eyed
Kateřina, she who rides the clouds of storm
And rains down her loving and giving. Née Frigga,
This mother of ten, purchases the food of gods
And strews the palaces with her cold disdain
Of illusion and imagination. She is the real
Daughter of Earth: in her hot blood, dreams
Melt and the beauty of what we see gleams
And what we touch burns like ice. Remember,
On Fridays, this female, the ferment she dispels
How, by the touch of her hand on your brow, sorrow
Dispels, calm descends, and, after her loving,
Sleep, like death, aimless and blank, drops down and down.

SATURDAY

I could always run rings around him, Rappaport
Kingston Gray, my lead-in-the-pants step-father.
He worked hard for a living, hustling soft-drinks.
Every payday, once a week, on Saturdays, he
Would breeze into town from the territory
Where he tacked up window displays and drank
Coca-Cola. Home he would sit dull and drink
Coca-Cola, while mother cooked the only meals worth
Eating all that week. He ate her confections
In silence, while I gabbled on to mother
And asked her how he felt. She always told me
"Tired." Those days I played by myself. Once
He took me to a football game an autumn afternoon.
The crowd, the tackles, the popcorn, the chill air
Drove me manic. He calmed me with a kick.
Now, he looks like Father Time and it is too easy
To use the thunderbolt of my pen to dethrone him.
What can I say? Tote up his mistakes and mine?
Little father, you were not there enough and I
Grew up alone. Look at me. I disgorge a stone.

SUNDAY

My first born, fairest child is 93 million miles away,
Anna The Good, who wants, first, to go to church,
Who wants, next, to rest like the Lord of Creation,
DingDong, in the mess of her beautiful eyes.
Her father, McMullen The Wise, scares her, his beard
Looks like the torn tangle of her mind. At table
She will not eat nor drink unless the wine
Is poured, the bread broken. How to resurrect
Her childishness, lead her back to the backyard
Where, one Sunday, on the 4th of July, five years old,
She danced, a sunsparkle, fire-sparklers dripping from her hands.
Tense she is now and waiting,
Seven years old of debate, will-she, nill-she.
She wants incest, I guess, with her father
And he, a master of transformation, speaks
An oracle: "Years from now, when you marry,
Think not of me, grave-gone and weary, but clasp
In your arms some beauty who looks like me,
Who will say a poem for your daughter, a poem
That is fair and wise and good and gay."

Cold Turkey was originally published in an edition of twenty-five hundred copies in November, 1969. The book was printed on Swallow Text Laid stock by the Regensteiner Publishing Enterprises and bound by the Chicago Book Manufacturers. The record included with this volume was pressed by Eva-Tone Records of Deerfield, Illinois. The book was designed by Michael Patrick O'Connor.